Some stories in this book first appeared
in *The Town Mouse and the Country Mouse*.

ISBN 0 86163 073 4

© Award Publications Limited 1983
Spring House, Spring Place
London NW5, England

Printed in Hungary

Town Mouse and Country Mouse
and other Stories

Illustrated
by
Rene Cloke

AWARD PUBLICATIONS — LONDON

THE TOWN MOUSE
AND THE COUNTRY MOUSE.

The Country Mouse had invited
the Town Mouse to pay him a visit.
"I'm sure the country air will
do you good," he told him, "and
you will enjoy the beautiful
scenery. The country food is
most nourishing and you will find
it a pleasant change after your
usual rich diet.
Do come."

So the Town Mouse packed his bag and picked up his
umbrella, for he never went very far without it; then
he put on his top hat and started off for the country.

He found the rough lanes rather uncomfortable
for walking, his feet were used to smooth pavements and
he didn't like getting them muddy.

He looked in surprise at
the flowers in the hedges and
wondered if they were good to
eat.

When he passed a village pond with a family of ducks swimming happily about, he stared at them in astonishment.

"Surely those are not the same birds which I find roasted in the larder," he murmured, "and, dear me, that must be a live rabbit!" as a young rabbit scuttled through the hedge.

At last he reached the
Country Mouse's cottage,
a snug little nest in a
cornfield.

"Must I climb up there?"
he asked, "is it safe?"

"Of course it is," laughed the Country Mouse,
"hand me your bag and hang your umbrella on a
cornstalk — you won't want it here!"

The Town Mouse clambered up
and his friend showed him
round his nest.

"I keep my store of food in this cupboard," he said proudly, "my brush and dust-pan in that corner.

I like to keep my nest tidy and put everything in the right place.

My clothes hang on this little peg; here is my bed of hay clippings and, see, I have made up one for you by the window."

The Town Mouse thought it was all rather small and cramped but, as he was a visitor, he just nodded and said —

"Very neatly and comfortably arranged."

"Now, sit down and rest," begged the Country Mouse, "you look tired out. We will have supper at once and you will soon feel better."

The Town Mouse brightened up on hearing this and looked on eagerly as the Country Mouse spread a little check table-cloth on a toadstool table.

He took a slice of apple and two rather dry peas from the cupboard, placed two acorn cups of water side by side and, with great pride, laid an ear of corn across the table.

"Come along," he called to the Town Mouse, "you may have the apple and we will share the corn and the peas."

The Town Mouse thought that it looked a very poor meal for two people but he was too polite to say so.

He ate the piece of apple, one of the peas and nibbled at the corn.

"Is this your usual supper?" he asked.

"Well," replied the Country Mouse, "apple *and* corn at the same meal is rather special but I felt sure you would be hungry."

The Town Mouse still felt hungry when supper was over and thought longingly of the larder where he spent a good deal of his time when in the town.

"We'll take a stroll across the fields before bedtime," suggested the Country Mouse, "the fresh air will make you sleep well."

The Town Mouse considered that he had had quite enough fresh air but thought it would be bad manners to say so.

His friend pointed out many things of interest as they went along.

"See how swiftly the butterflies and dragonflies dash about," he said.

"You should see the cars and buses that go thundering down the streets in the town," replied the Town Mouse, "that would make your hair stand on end."

The Country Mouse thought that this wouldn't be very comfortable but agreed that it must be quite exciting.

Their walk took them past a field where a friendly cow gave such a loud moo over the hedge that the Town Mouse jumped with fright.

"Tell me," he squealed, "is that creature dangerous? Might it come into the cornfield and trample down your cottage?"

"No fear of that!" laughed the Country Mouse, "the farmer keeps the gate tightly closed."

In spite of the fresh air, the Town Mouse didn't sleep very well; he still felt hungry and he worried a good deal about the cow.

The Country Mouse was up at sunrise.

He tidied the nest and put a few berries and the remaining grains of corn on the table.

"Breakfast is ready," he called out, "I hope you are fond of fruit."

The Town Mouse rubbed his sleepy eyes and looked at the table.

"Fruit!" he murmured, thinking sadly of the choice pears and peaches he was used to nibbling in the larder at home. However, he did not want to hurt his friend's feelings by showing that he thought that this was a poor sort of breakfast, so he praised the flavour of the berries.

"I think I must make my way home," he said when there was nothing left on the table, "my visit has been most — er — interesting; I shall have a good deal to think about and my friends will be very eager to hear of my adventures."

The Country Mouse looked disappointed.

"I hoped you would stay a little longer," he said, "I had planned a long walk to-day and you haven't seen the view from the top of the haystack.

"You can see across the fields to the farmyard and watch the swallows feeding their young ones in the barn. There hasn't been time to show you the river where the kingfisher and the water vole live."

"You are most kind," answered the Town Mouse, hurrying down the cornstalk and collecting his umbrella, "but you must certainly come and visit me soon.

I will show you all the sights of the town and you must join my friends in a grand banquet."

This sounded most exciting and the Country Mouse said he was delighted to accept the invitation.

"Come along with me now," suggested the Town Mouse, "we shall be company for each other on the long walk."

So the Country Mouse bundled his belongings into a spotted handkerchief and the two friends started off together for the big town.

First along the country lanes and through the wood, then down the village street where they had to be wary of cats and dogs.

It was getting dark by the time they reached the house where the Town Mouse lived.

The Country Mouse was rather scared at the traffic; it was so noisy and dashed past them so quickly that he felt quite bewildered.

"Is it always so busy?" he asked "or perhaps there is a Fair to-day," for a Fair was the busiest thing he had ever seen.

The Town Mouse laughed. "Don't be nervous," he answered, "just follow me," and he scampered and disappeared into a hole.

The Country Mouse followed him along a dark passage and found himself in the basement kitchen of a large house.

"Quick!" whispered the Town Mouse, "I hear the cook coming!"

They had just time to scuttle into a hole in the skirting-board as the cook rushed at them with a soup ladle.

"Mice again!" he cried, "I shall have to set a trap."

The two mice had to wait until midnight before the kitchen was
quiet and then they crept out and made their way to the larder.

On the shelves they found a number of mice already nibbling
at the food there.

There were joints of meat, fruit, jellies, cakes and cheese.

"This is my friend from the country," said the Town Mouse,
"I have been paying him a visit and now I want him to see some
town life. Try some of this delicious cheese, my dear fellow,
it is quite harmless as long as it isn't baiting a trap!"

The Country Mouse had found the traffic
and the cook's threat of a trap so
frightening that he wished he could be
home again in the cornfield but all
the mice greeted him kindly so he
joined the feast.

The cheese was good and so was the
fruit but the other food seemed much
too rich and he really felt too nervous
to have a good appetite.

"Miau-o-o!"

"That cat again!" squealed the mice and in a moment they had all vanished under the floor boards.

"This life wouldn't suit me," declared the Country Mouse to himself and he hid behind an apple as the cat looked round the door, "it may be full of thrills and excitements and there is certainly plenty to eat, but I prefer a quiet life without so many dangers.

Thank you for the delicious feast," he called out — "Good-bye, all!"

He picked up his hat and bundle, made his way out of the kitchen and started for home.

How good it was to feel the fresh air
again!

The Country Mouse made his way bravely
along the busy streets, hiding from
prowling cats and dogs and dodging the
traffic

He reached his nest in the cornfield
as the dawn was breaking and gazed out
at the view.

"How beautiful it is!" he sighed as
he nibbled an ear of corn, "I shall
never want to roam again!"

THE DOG, THE COCK
AND THE FOX

A dog and a cock agreed to make their home together.

At night, the cock flew into the branches of a tree to roost while the dog curled up in the hollow trunk.

In the morning a fox, passing by, decided that he would like to eat the cock for his breakfast and asked him to come down and have a chat.

"Certainly," answered the cock, "just knock on the trunk and wake my friend who will let you in."

So the fox rapped on the tree trunk but out rushed the dog who very soon killed him.

THE FOX AND THE GRAPES

"Those grapes look delicious," said a hungry fox looking up at a bunch of fine grapes, "what a pity they are growing so high."

He jumped and jumped but however hard he tried, he couldn't get quite high enough.

At last he lost his temper and walked away. "I shan't bother about them any more," he muttered, "they look nice but they are probably sour!"

THE LION AND THE MOUSE

A lion was having a sleep when a mouse ran over his paws and the lion awoke with a mighty roar.

"How dare you disturb me!" he growled, catching the mouse in his great paw.

"Please spare me!" squeaked the mouse, "the day may come when I will be able to save your life!"

This sounded so stupid that the lion laughed and let the mouse go.

A little while later, the lion was caught in a net which some hunters had spread to catch him and the mouse, finding him struggling, ran to help him.

He gnawed at the ropes with his sharp little teeth and very soon the lion was free.

"How glad I am that I spared your life," said the lion, "for now you have saved mine."

THE COCK AND THE JEWEL

A cock was scratching the ground and looking for something to eat when he dug up a piece of sparkling jewellery.

"Very fine," he said, turning it over, "but no good to me.

I would much rather have found a grain of corn!"

THE WOLF AND THE GOAT

"Why don't you come down here where the grass is greener?" the sly wolf called to the goat.

"Thank you," replied the goat, who felt safer up on the rocks, "but if I come down to get a good meal, you will make a good meal of me. I would rather eat the poorer grass in safety."

THE GRASSHOPPER AND
THE ANT

The grasshopper laughed at the ant who was busy collecting food for her winter store.

"Why don't you enjoy life as I am doing?" he asked as he played a merry tune on his banjo.

"You will be sorry when winter comes and you have no food," replied the ant.

When the winter did come, the grasshopper was very sorry for himself and begged the ant for a grain of corn from her store.

"You played and sang all the summer," answered the ant, "now you can dance," and she rather unkindly slammed the door.

THE DOG AND HIS BONE

Toby had been given a lovely meaty bone by a friendly butcher.

"I'll hurry home with this", he said to himself, "I hope I won't meet any other dogs on the way."

He scampered off down the lane watched by some young rabbits who were not at all interested in bones.

"What a strange thing to eat!" they said to each other, "we would much rather have a nice fresh lettuce or a bunch of radishes."

Toby ran across the fields to where a bridge crossed the river.

Holding his bone tightly, he peered into the water. „That's a funny meal!" laughed a fat frog, "a few worms or insects would be much tastier."

Toby took no notice for he thought he could see another dog with a bone standing in the water.

"He has a bigger bone than mine," declared greedy Toby and, dropping his own bone, he dived into the river hoping to snatch the bone from the other dog.

But it was only his own reflection and it disappeared as Toby splashed into the water.

"Now I haven't got either bone," he whimpered as he scrambled out of the river.

THE HARE AND THE TORTOISE

The Hare laughed as he watched the Tortoise plodding along.

"It must take you a very long time to get anywhere," he jeered, "I could run to the other end of the field and back while you are crossing the road!"

"Your legs may be longer than mine," answered the Tortoise who was tired of being teased, "but I get along in my own good time."

This made the Hare laugh so the Tortoise declared angrily that he would challenge the Hare to a race.

Their friends marked out a distance across the field and through the wood.

"It won't be a very exciting race," said the Squirrel, "Hare is sure to win."

"I expect Tortoise will reach the winning post some day next week," said the Rabbits.

The little Mice thought it was a big joke and hurried off to the winning post to see the finish of the race.

Old Owl started off the two runners with a loud "Hoot-toot!" and off went Hare at a fine pace.

When he reached the wood, he decided to sit down and have a rest.

"No need to worry," he murmured, "it will take Tortoise all day to get as far as this."

It was a warm day and Hare was soon fast asleep in the sunshine.

While he slept, Tortoise crept steadily by and plodded on through the wood.

When the Hare awoke, he looked around for the Tortoise.

"No sign of him yet," he laughed, "I'd better run along and finish the race."

But, when he came to the winning post, he was very annoyed to hear all the animals cheering the Tortoise, who had arrived a minute earlier.

"Slow and steady wins the race," remarked the Tortoise.

THE STAG AT THE POOL

A Stag went to a pool in the forest to drink and looked at his reflection in the water.

"What a splendid pair of antlers I have," he said, "but I am ashamed of my thin legs."

Just then, a Lion roared and the Stag bounded away, his thin legs carrying him to safety.

But, alas! running beneath a tree, his fine antlers were caught in its branches and the Lion was able to catch him.

"My despised legs would have saved me," moaned the Stag, "but my fine antlers have been my ruin."

THE FOX AND
THE CROW

The Crow was sitting in a tree enjoying a large piece of cheese when the Fox passed by.

"That looks good," the Fox said to himself, "but, as I can't climb trees, I must use my wits to get it for myself."

He sat beneath the tree.

"Good morning Mr. Crow, how well you look! Your wings have such a gloss in the sunshine and your beak is so handsomely curved! I expect your voice is just as beautiful as you are."

The silly Crow felt very flattered
and, opening his beak, he gave a loud
ugly — "Caw!"

The cheese fell to the ground and,
in a moment, the Fox grabbed it and
bounded away.

"You certainly have a fine voice,"
declared the Fox, "but you are not very clever!"

THE MICE IN COUNCIL

The Mice were very worried.

"The Cat is becoming a great danger," said one, "there won't be many of us left soon."

"We must hold a meeting," said another, "and think out a plan to keep us in safety."

So the Mice met that evening but, although they talked for a long time, no-one had any really good ideas.

At last, one young mouse stood up.

"I think I have a good plan," he announced proudly, "we must tie a bell around the cat's neck and by it's ringing we shall know when she is near."

"Hear! hear!" cried all the other Mice, "that's a splendid idea!"

The oldest Mouse got to his feet.

"The plan sounds a very good one," said he, "but who, may I ask, is going to put a bell on the Cat?"